Flan Across the River

NICK WARBURTON

Illustrated by John Rogan

OXFORD

UNIVERSITY PRESS

OXFORD

UNIVERSITY PRESS

Great Clarendon Street, Oxford OX2 6DP

Oxford University Press is a department of the University of Oxford.
It furthers the University's objective of excellence in research, scholarship,
and education by publishing worldwide in

Oxford   New York

Auckland   Cape Town   Dar es Salaam   Hong Kong   Karachi
Kuala Lumpur   Madrid   Melbourne   Mexico City   Nairobi
New Delhi   Shanghai   Taipei   Toronto

With offices in

Argentina   Austria   Brazil   Chile   Czech Republic   France   Greece
Guatemala   Hungary   Italy   Japan   Poland   Portugal   Singapore
South Korea   Switzerland   Thailand   Turkey   Ukraine   Vietnam

Oxford is a registered trade mark of Oxford University Press
in the UK and in certain other countries

First published 1995
This edition 2005

British Library Cataloguing in Publication Data
Data available

ISBN-13: 978-0-19-917978-7
ISBN-10: 0-19-917978-6

1 3 5 7 9 10 8 6 4 2

Available in packs
Stage 11 Pack of 6:
ISBN-13: 978-0-19-917973-2; ISBN-10: 0-19-917973-5
Stage 11 Class Pack:
ISBN-13: 978-0-19-917980-0; ISBN-10: 0-19-917980-8
Guided Reading Cards also available:
ISBN-13: 978-0-19-917982-4; ISBN-10: 0-19-917982-4

Cover artwork by Bill Bolton
Photograph of Nick Warburton © Eaden Lilley Photography, Cambridge

Printed in China by Imago

Flan trouble

'Rodney!'

Mr Bodney the baker dusted the flour from his hands and called for his son. His son, Rodney, was snoozing in a chair by the big oven. Mr Bodney tweaked his ear and woke him up.

'Listen,' he said, 'I want you to take five sticky, syrupy flans to Mr Crab's shop.'

'Right-oh, Dad,' said Rodney, yawning. 'Mr Crab's shop, on the other side of the river.'

'Yes, and don't dawdle and don't daydream or I'll go up the wall. Mr Crab doesn't want these flans tomorrow. He wants them today.'

'Yes, Dad,' said Rodney. 'Leave it to me.'

He tucked the box of flans under his arm and set off for Mr Crab's shop. He walked along the river bank until he came to the wooden bridge. Or rather, he came to the place where the bridge used to be. And his mouth fell open. The bridge had collapsed. The middle part had fallen in the river and floated away.

'Now what am I going to do?' he said.

5

Mr Crab came out of his shop on the other side of the river and called across to him.

'Have you got my flans, Rodney?' he shouted.

Rodney looked at the river swirling by and he looked at the box of sticky, syrupy flans.

'I've got them here, Mr Crab,' he shouted.

'I don't want them there,' called Mr
Crab. 'I want them here.'

'I can't cross the river without a
bridge,' thought Rodney. Then he had
an idea.

'Just coming, Mr Crab,' he said. 'I'll
use the box as a boat and float the
flans across. Get ready.'

Rodney put the box of flans on the water and held his breath.

'It'll be awful if they sink,' he said to himself.

The flans didn't sink. They bobbed out into the river like a little boat.

'Clever,' said Rodney to himself.

But at that moment the box swirled in the current and flans began to float downstream. Then some ducks plunged into the river after them. The ducks made such a noise that several more people joined Mr Crab on the other side of the river. They wanted to see what all the fuss was about.

Rodney ran along the river bank,
trying to keep up with the floating
flans. He grabbed a stick and managed
to steer the box back to the shore. By
then, though, the ducks had pecked
one of the flans away to nothing.

'Now look what you've done,'
Rodney said to the ducks. 'I've only got
four left. And Dad will go up the wall.'

The ducks paddled about, watching
Rodney to see what he would do next.
Rodney didn't know what to do, so he
sat down on the bank and thought.

As he sat there, Rodney noticed that
a stiff breeze was blowing. It was
blowing across the river towards Mr
Crab's shop.

'Of course,' he thought. 'I'll sail
them across.'

Not very clever

Rodney jumped up and took off his
shirt. Using the stick as a mast, he
made a sail for the box of syrupy flans.
The box was quite soggy after its first
trip, so Rodney only floated one flan
out onto the river.

The wind caught the shirt-tail and the box began to move across the river. Rodney heard some cheering from the other bank. Quite a crowd had gathered outside Mr Crab's shop.

The ducks quacked and set off after the box.

'Very clever,' Rodney told himself when it was half way across.

Then the wind dropped. The little boat stopped sailing and Rodney's shirt dragged in the water. Rodney tried to puff at it from his side of the river but he knew it was no good. The box began to bob away down the river with the ducks paddling after it as fast they could go.

'Oh no!' cried the crowd.

Rodney sat down and thought again.
He looked at the three flans that were
left. Then he looked at the other shore.

It was too far to throw a flan, he
thought, but a kick might do it.

'It's worth a try,' he cried, jumping to
his feet.

'He's going to kick it,' yelled someone
from the crowd.

Three or four more people came
running up to watch.

Rodney held one of the flans in front
of him. He dropped it and swung his
foot as hard as he could. The crowd
shouted with excitement and a little
dog barked.

It was such a strong kick that it
lifted Rodney clean off the ground. But
the flan did not fly into the air. It
made a loud splat and stuck to
Rodney's foot.

The crowd across the river laughed
out loud.

'Oh dear,' said Rodney, wiping syrup from his bare chest. 'I must find a way of getting flans over the river without exploding them first.'

Then he remembered his stretchy belt. If he fixed it to the branch of a tree, he could make a catapult. If he shot a flan from a catapult, it might not explode.

'Really very clever,' he told himself.

It look him some minutes to fix his belt to a nearby tree. It wasn't easy because his trousers kept slipping down. In the end, he had to take them off altogether. The crowd clapped and cheered to see him skipping about in his stripy pants.

When the catapult was ready,
Rodney pulled the belt back as far as it
would go, He had to lean back as far as
it would go. He had to lean back in the
grass to do it.

'Three – two – one – FIRE!' shouted
the crowd and Rodney let go of the belt.

The flan went spinning high over the
water like a discus.

'Look out, Mr Crab,' Rodney called.
'Flan on its way!'

This time the flan cleared the river. It hung in the air for a moment and the crowd waited ready to catch it. Down it came and everyone ran forward with their arms out.

'Mine! Mine!' called Mr Crab.

Then Mr Crab stumbled over the little dog and sat down on the bank with a thump.

'Oh no,' said Rodney, and closed his eyes.

Rodney heard a loud slap as the flan landed. Then he heard the crowd cheer. When Rodney opened his eyes, Mr Crab was sitting there with the flan on his head like a floppy hat.

'Don't worry, Mr Crab,' Rodney called. 'There's one flan left and I'm sure I can get it to you all right. Don't go away.'

But the crowd was now so big
that Mr Crab couldn't go away if he
wanted to.

One last chance, thought Rodney, or
Dad really will go up the wall.

He picked up his trousers and tied a
knot in each of the legs. Then he took
some string from his pockets. He began
to tie it round the last flan.

'What's he up to this time?' shouted
a man on the other side of the river.

Flan-tastic!

'It's a parachute,' someone answered.

'Rodney Bodney's making a parachute with his trousers!'

And that's just what Rodney was doing. He wrapped the flan carefully in his trousers and stretched his belt as far as it would go.

'THREE – TWO – ONE – FIRE!' yelled the crowd.

Off went the flan and the crowd gasped.

'Oooh... Aarh!'

The flan began to tumble out of the sky. It fell down like a stone.

'LOOK OUT!' shouted the crowd and everyone ducked.

Then the trousers filled with air. They became as fat as two balloons and floated slowly, rocking from side to side, towards the ground. The flan dropped gently into Mr Crab's waiting arms, and an even louder cheer went up.

'He's done it!' yelled a voice. 'Three cheers for Rodney Bodney. Hip-hip...'

'Hoor-RAY!'

Everyone was glad that the flan had landed safely. Everyone but Rodney. He turned away and went home feeling sorry for himself.

Four sticky syrupy flans, a shirt and a pair of good trousers – all lost. Not at all clever. And what was Dad going to say?

When he got home he found Mr Bodney waiting for him at the bakery door. Rodney felt foolish standing there in nothing by his stripy pants. He looked down and saw smudges of sticky syrup on his chest and legs.

He was sure that Mr Bodney was about to go right up the wall. But the baker was smiling.

'Mr Crab has just been on the phone,' he said to Rodney.

'Ah yes,' said Rodney, swallowing hard. 'I can explain about that. I really did try my best...'

'He wants to thank you for the flan,' Mr Bodney went on. 'He says he's had a wonderful morning.'

Rodney could hardly believe his ears. He was sure that Mr Crab would be hopping mad with him.

'A wonderful morning?' he said.

'Yes,' said Mr Bodney. 'He says he's never seen such a crowd before. They've been in and out of his shop all morning. And all because of you.'

'Well,' said Rodney, smiling with relief, 'I did my very best.'

Mr Bodney smiled too, and patted his son on the back.

'Mr Crab wants you to deliver five more sticky, syrupy flans for him tomorrow,' he said. 'Just the same as today.'

About the author

While I was teaching, I enjoyed drama and reading books aloud with children. This encouraged me to write and since then I have written a number of scripts for radio, stage and television, around a baker's  dozen or so – that is, thirteen – children's books. I do like sticky, syrupy flans and buns too, although I can't ever remember inventing anything.

I enjoy reading, almost anything to do with cricket, and cycling around Cambridge, where I live with my family.